© 2016, Sebnem Nehir

SUPERSTAR FRUITS AND VEGETABLES IN THE QURAN

Written and Illustrated by
Seyma Mert

Edited by
Sebnem Nehir

Translated by
Hilal Bayramoglu

Edited and Translated by
Krenare Aliovski

Activities from
Sebnem Nehir

Sebnem Nehir Hadith Craft Packages

hadispaketleri@gmail.com
www.facebook.com/hadispaketleri
Visit Sebnem Nehir YouTube Channel!

Superstar Fruits and Vegetables in the Quran

I do not have apple or fig trees, vineyards and beehives. But I would love to play tag with cherries, draw smiles on bananas and even build a tower out of pomegranates.

Did you know all of these fruits are mentioned in the Holy Quran? Allah (Subhanahu Wa Ta'Ala) has created all of the fruits and vegetables in the world and each of them have their own unique shape, taste and colour. Fruits and vegetables give us the vitamins we need to make us grow big and strong!

I wrote this book because I wanted to thank Allah (Subhanahu Wa Ta'Ala) for providing us with all of the fruits and vegetables through which we receive the nutrients we need to live a healthy life! While you read about these superstar fruits you will also want to thank Allah (Subhanahu Wa Ta'Ala).

Fruitful reading,

Seyma Mert

What does Allah (Subhanahu Wa Ta'Ala) reveal to us in the Holy Quran?

In Surah Al-'An'am (The Cattle) [6: 99] -

"And it is He who sends down rain from the sky, and We produce thereby the growth of all things. We produce from it greenery from which We produce grains arranged in layers. And from the palm trees - of its emerging fruit are clusters hanging low. And [We produce] gardens of grapevines and olives and pomegranates, similar yet varied. Look at [each of] its fruit when it yields and [at] its ripening. Indeed in that are signs for a people who believe."

What does our Prophet Muhammed (Peace Be Upon Him) reveal to us?

"My Lord! Grant us Your blessings in our fruits, and Your blessings for our city. Grant us Your blessings in our measures."

(Ibn Majah, Tirmidhi).

THE SMILING BANANA

Sometimes, I am so active in class and consume all my energy at school that once I get home I feel completely exhausted. It made me wonder how monkeys are always so energetic. They swing free tree to tree and run through their habitat. Could it be because they eat bananas?

You can draw a monkey swinging HERE!

I heard that bananas are a delicious source of protein and potassium. That must be where monkeys get all their energy! Bananas make great snack to help me have strong bones.

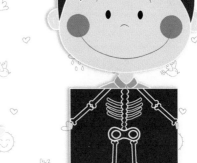

Did you know that bananas are mentioned in the Holy Quran? Just looking at a banana makes me happy because they are shaped in the form of a smile! Bananas provide us with energy that cheers us up. Perhaps this is why monkeys are also so cheerful!

4

What does Allah (Subhanahu Wa Ta'Ala) reveal to us in the Holy Quran?

In Surah Waqia (The Inevitable) [56: 28-33] -

"[They will be] among lote trees with thorns removed, and [banana] trees layered [with fruit], and shade extended, and water poured out, and fruit, abundant [and varied], neither limited [to season] nor forbidden."

FUN FRUITY FACTS

Bananas are not all yellow in colour; some may be green, brown or red.

Bananas are made up of 75% water. If a banana was a pool instead of a fruit, we could swim in it!

Colour bananas!

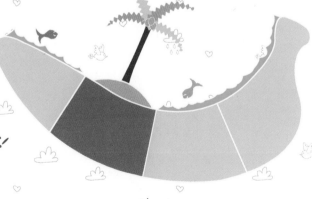

Did you know bananas do not grow on trees? They grow on 2-3 meter long, treelike plants.

Did you know that most bananas are grown in India? Banana lovers let's take a trip to India!

THE JAZZY CHERRY

Sometimes I think about how fruits can resemble other things. This is sometimes how I come up with ideas for stories. One day for instance, I was wondering why cherries are worn as earrings.

A long time ago, the people that first discovered the cherry thought that they looked like earrings. They would hang the bright red cherries on their ears but noticed that the fruit only lasted a few days before they began to fade. Instead of wearing the cherries as earrings, they decided to taste them. The cherries were so sweet and delicious that everyone decided to eat their cherry earrings!

Can you draw cherry earrings to me?

Draw lines to match the same color cherries.

Bananas and cherries are both sweet in taste. These fruits are both mentioned in Surah Waqia (The Inevitable), we should be so thankful that Allah (Subhanahu Wa Ta'Ala) for these delicious fruits!

Draw a happy face to my cherry HERE!

What does Allah (Subhanahu Wa Ta'Ala) reveal to us in the Holy Quran?

In Surah Waqia (The Inevitable) [56: 28-33] –

"[They will be] among lote trees with thorns removed, and [banana] trees layered [with fruit], and shade extended, and water poured out, and fruit, abundant [and varied], neither limited [to season] nor forbidden."

FUN FRUITY FACTS

Cherries are completely tooth-friendly. They strive to make our teeth healthy.

Besides humans, birds like cherries too! You might see birds stop and rest on a cherry tree to enjoy a snack!

The cherry tree also has health benefits. Its barks are good for lowering a fever and its flowers can sooth a cough.

Cherries like cleanliness so much, that they make our blood spick and span. Good for them!

NOTE FROM THE AUTHOR!

There are different kinds of cherries; some are red, orange and even yellow in colour. Cherries are usually sweet in taste, however there are also sour cherries! Sour cherries are a luminous red colour and smaller in size. Make sure to buy the sweet ones at the grocery store or you'll be in for a sour surprise!

THE GROOVY GRAPE

This morning, my little brother and I played our favourite guessing game.

We each took a turn at tasting fruit with our eyes closed and had to guess the fruit! Even with my eyes closed, I always guess grapes correctly! Grapes are shaped like mini spheres, and provide a burst of juice when you bite into them!

How many grapes are in this picture?

Write down the number HERE!

↓

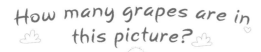

What if all fruit had the same taste, colour and shape? Then how would we tell the difference between all these delicious fruit? Especially juicy grapes, I wouldn't change their yummy taste for any other fruit! Luckily, Allah (Subhanahu Wa Ta'Ala) has created this delicious fruit for us. Did you know that the grape is mentioned exactly 12 times in our Holy Book, the Quran. The Quran reveals that grapes and vineyards have been created especially for us, aren't we so lucky?

What does Allah (Subhanahu Wa Ta'Ala) reveal to us in the Holy Quran?

In Surah An-Nahl (The Bee)
[16: 11] -

> "He causes to grow for you thereby the crops, olives, palm trees, grapevines, and from all the fruits. Indeed in that is a sign for a people who give thought."

FUN FRUITY FACTS

It's estimated that there are approximately 15,000 kinds of grapes in the world that provide our brain and body with tons of energy! I wonder if grapes know all of their relatives? I should ask!

It is said that grapes come in a variety of colours such as red, yellow, green...You don't expect me to count all the colors now, do you!

The grape is the most popular fruit after the orange. So what is the most popular then? Come on, I told you! Here's a hint: the orange! I guess that was more than just a hint!

Look at the pattern. Circle grapes that continue the pattern.

Look at the numbers in grapes. Each row adds up to 20. Find the missing numbers in some grapes.

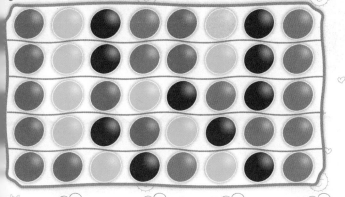

8   1   0   4   3
  3   2   5   1
    11 1   7
      5   9
        18
        20

LET'S COUNT FRUITS!

Count each kind of fruit and fill your answers below.

How many ? _22_   How many 🍒 ? _____

How many ● ? _____   How many ? _____

10

HOW TALL ARE THEY?

Measure each type of fruit, then write how many inches tall in the boxes.

6

THE POMPOM POMEGRANATE

Pomegranate is not as easy to peel as the banana. If you want to eat a piece of pomegranate, you should ask an elder to split it in half for you. After the pomegranate is halved, its red seeds are revealed.

HALF CUT POMEGRANATE!

WHOLE POMEGRANATE!

There are white transparent membranes on attached to the red seeds. Rid the tiny pomegranate seeds from those membranes before you eat them! You can do this putting the seeds in a plate and then filling the plate with water. This way, the membranes stay on the surface of the water and the edible fruit can sink to the bottom. When you pour the water into the sink, your fruit is ready to munch on!

=1/1 =1/3 =1/5 =1/2 =1/4

The pomegranate is also mentioned in the Holy Quran. How nice that **Allah** (Subhanahu Wa Ta'Ala) has created the pomegranate fruit for us...

I drank half of my pomegranate juice. Which glass is my juice?

Hey! Not so fast, where did the entire pomegranate go? Did you finish eating without me? You finish the story; it's my turn to snack on pomegranate!

What does Allah (Subhanahu Wa Ta'Ala) reveal to us in the Holy Quran?

In Surah Al-'An'am (The Cattle) [6: 141] –

"It is He Who produceth gardens, with trellises and without, and dates, and tilth with produce of all kinds, and olives and pomegranates, similar (in kind) and different (in variety): eat of their fruit in their season, but render the dues that are proper on the day that the harvest is gathered. But waste not by excess: for Allah (Subhanahu Wa Ta'Ala) loveth not the wasters."

FUN FRUITY FACTS

Pomegranate seeds are delicious on salads, Noah's pudding, or rose pudding.

Write the numbers of pomegranates into the spaces.

Colour the spaces with a number **1** to RED.

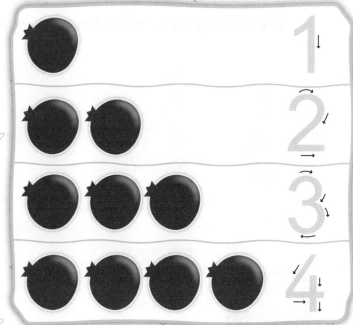

Pomegranates with its minerals and vitamins save our heart. There are so much fruits to do so. Then, that means our heart needs to be saved. Let's eat plenty of fruits to save it!

THE SWEET DATE

Some fruits grow in specific climates. Can you guess which fruit grows in one of the hottest climates? It's the date, of course! Dates thrive in the hot heat. If the weather is not warm enough, they refuse to grow! It's easy to get dehydrated if you sit out in the sun. This is why dates also love water. Water and sunshine help dates grow.

Which date drank more water?   Circle the most biggest date!

Did you know that the date tree and it's fruit are mentioned in the Holy Quran 20 times! Dates are very beneficial to our health and contain a bunch of nutrients that help us grow. We should be so thankful that Allah (Subhanahu Wa Ta'Ala) has created such sweet tasting fruit for us to enjoy.

Can you count all the dates, suns and water drops in 50 seconds?
Let's start!

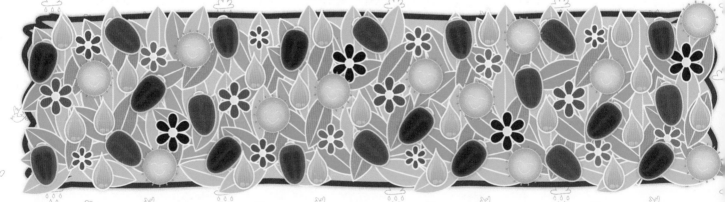

How many dates are there? _____   How many suns are there? _____

How many water drops are there? _____

What does Allah (Subhanahu Wa Ta'Ala) reveal to us in the Holy Quran?

In Surah Al-Mu'minun (The Believers) [23: 19] –

"And We brought forth for you thereby gardens of palm trees and grapevines in which for you are abundant fruits and from which you eat."

FUN FRUITY FACTS

Dates contain almost all the vitamins, proteins and minerals we need to stay healthy!

Dates are especially beneficial to the health our heart, bones, lungs and eyes.

If I had to choose 3 things to take with me on a deserted island, one of them would surely be dates because they would provide me with nutrition!

Draw HERE!

What would you take to a deserted island?

THE ITTY BITTY FIG

We went out to do shopping with mummy this morning. While we were walking and moving into deep conversation, I catched a great scent. But it was the first time that I smelt such this. I stopped and looked around.

What did we buy from the grocery store? I am giving you the first letters. Circle the fruits and write them!

A

D

O

F

We were under a tree. As I raised my head, I saw green fruits on the branches. Are those apples? No. Then plums? No. I looked at the ground and there was a fallen fruitlet right in front of my foot. Oops only then I recognized it. To my surprise, the scent belonged to the fig tree.

I met the fig tree in our street just this morning. From now on, we may say hi and ask him how he is. There is a surah called "The Fig" in our lovely book, Quran. It's original name is "Tin" and it means fig in Arabic. How do I know that, huh? Of course I searched about it. I like searching then learning. Because I am as curious as every child!

What does Allah (Subhanahu Wa Ta'Ala) reveal to us in the Holy Quran?

In Surah At-Tin (The Fig) [95: 1-4]

"By the Fig and the Olive, and the Mount of Sinai, And [by] this secure city [Makkah], We have certainly created man in the best of stature."

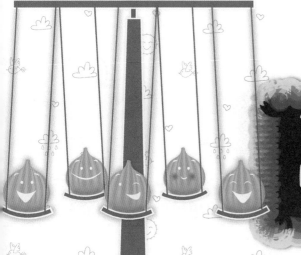

FUN FRUITY FACTS

Turkey is the world's leading fig producer. Thank you Turkey!

Figs can be made into a jam, molasses, puree or the base of a dessert. We are so efficient with the way we use our figs!

Can you try to write the word "fig" in Arabic?

Start from HERE!

تين

Figs can be eaten fresh or dry. They do not last long as fresh fruit, which is why they are often eaten as dried fruit.

Figs provide your hair with nutrients that help it grow.

COUNT AND CLASSIFY

Can you answer the questions below?

HOW MANY?

Are fruits? _____

Are vegetables? _____

Are orange? _____

Are red? _____

Are purple? _____

Are green? _____

Are brown? _____

Are pink? _____

Grow on trees? _____

COUNT AND COLOUR

Colour the correct number of fruits!

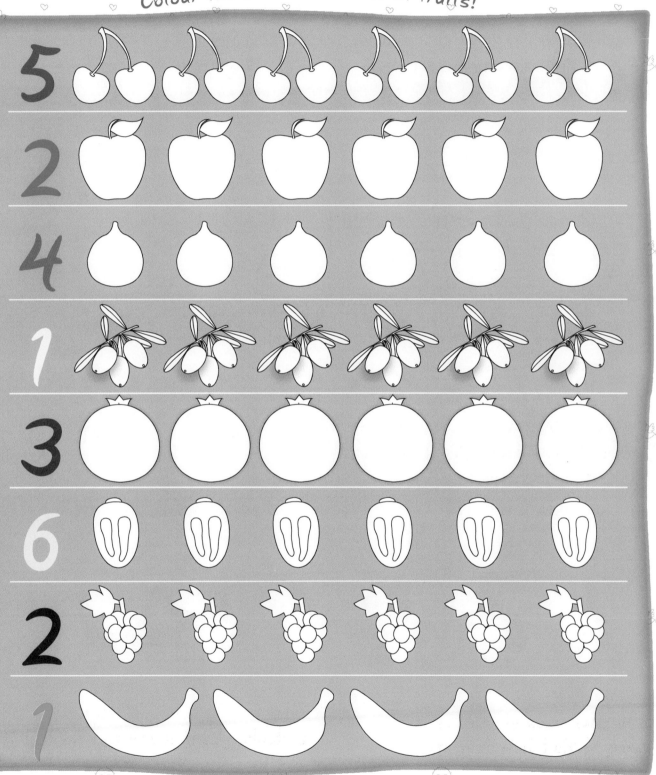

MY HUCKLEBERRY FRIEND THE APPLE

The history of the apple is quite interesting. My great, great grandfather knew a lot about apples. One day told me a story from Prophet Joseph's day. Prophet Joseph was a really handsome man, so handsome that those who saw him in public were awestruck. Sometimes, as while they were busy cutting apples, they would stare at him instead and accidently cut themselves!

I want to match my apples. But my lines got tangled up.

Can you help me?

Knives are dangerous, so I suggest you enjoy apples by biting into them! Apples are also mentioned in the Holy Quran.

Thank you **Allah** (Subhanahu Wa Ta'Ala) for providing us with apples!

Can you match the pairs to make six apples?

What does Allah (Subhanahu Wa Ta'Ala) reveal to us in the Holy Quran?

In Surah An-Nahl (The Bee) [16: 11] -

"He causes to grow for you thereby the crops, olives, palm trees, grapevines, and from all the fruits. Indeed in that is a sign for a people who give thought."

FUN FRUITY FACTS

Horses, monkeys, chimpanzees, bears, raccoons, and rabbits like apples too. Horses, especially love to munch on apples.

Megatons of apples are produced every year.

Did you know China is the leading producer of apples? Thank you China!

Help the worm to find it's way out of apple.

Apples do not sink when you throw them into a bowl of water because they have air. Maybe we can use them to float in water?

Apples keep our teeth clean and shiny!

THE TINY OLIVE

Would you consider the olive to be a fruit or a vegetable? When I was asked this question, I replied that the olive is neither. To my surprise it turned out the olive is a fruit!

Circle the fruits!

Olives are not the type of fruit that can be picked and eaten off the tree. Olives have a bitter taste when they are ripe. They mus be put in water and salt to remove their bitter taste. I didn't realize what an extensive process it was to make olives ready to eat. Now I appreciate them more!

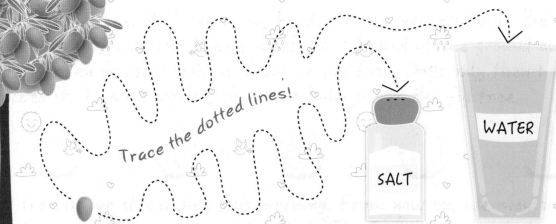

Trace the dotted lines!

SALT

WATER

The olive is mentioned 6 times in the Holy Quran. Olives are also the key ingredient in olive oil that you put on salad. Did you know olive oil is mentione 2 times in the Holy Quran? Olives and olive oil must be very nutritious!

What does Allah (Subhanahu Wa Ta'Ala) reveal to us in the Holy Quran?

In Surah An-Nahl (The Bee) [16: 17] -

"He causes to grow for you thereby the crops, olives, palm trees, grapevines, and from all the fruits. Indeed in that is a sign for a people who give thought."

FUN FRUITY FACTS

Olive trees never shed their leaves and their leaves always stay green.

Olive trees last approximately 2000 years. I am sure that a 2000 years old olive tree has so much to tell!

Olives are green and then turn purple or black in colour. Green and black olives grow on the same tree and they change in colour afterwards.

Colour the olive branch!

Olive oil prevents hair loss and makes your hair healthy and shiny.

THE SOBBY ONION

Onions can be so emotional! Every time my mom cuts an onion, I notice her start to tear up. It's as if the onion is trying to make my mom cry! Once she starts to chop the onion, I hear her sniffling her nose and holding back her tears. One day I decided to stand up to the onion. "Stop making my mom cry!" I said staring at the onion. I noticed my eyes started to cry as well.

Who chopped an onion? Check the boxes!

My mom loves onion and puts it in a lot of our meals. I finally decided to ask her why if it makes her cry while chopping them. She told me that the onion has a very particular taste and adds a lot of flavour to our food. Without onion, those recipes would lose their charm! It is so interesting how the onion can add so much flavour to a dish but also make people emotional. Onions seem so talented, and they are also mentioned in the Holy Quran, that's how we know they must have an important purpose!

How many onions are there? Count them in 10 seconds! _____

What does Allah (Subhanahu Wa Ta'Ala) reveal to us in the Holy Quran?

In Surah Al-Baqarah (The Cow)
[02: 67] –

"And [recall] when you said, 'O Moses, we can never endure one [kind of] food. So call upon your Lord to bring forth for us from the earth its green herbs and its cucumbers and its garlic and its lentils and its onions'…"

FUN FRUITY FACTS

When an onion is cut, it produces a gas into the air. As a reaction, our eyes cry or get watery as a form of protection against the gas.

Can you match each sum with the correct answer?

Onions are a great form of nutrition and help you get etter if you are feeling sick.

Onions help increase your appetite.

Onions have a strong taste and stench that can be eased through a bite of bread!

25

NUMBER MAZE

Can you help the date get to Qabah? Draw a path from the date to Qabah by counting from 1 to 20.

FRUIT MIX-UP

These fruits are all mixed up. Can you put them back together? Cut out the pictures. Match them to make an apple, fig, banana, date, cherry and olives.

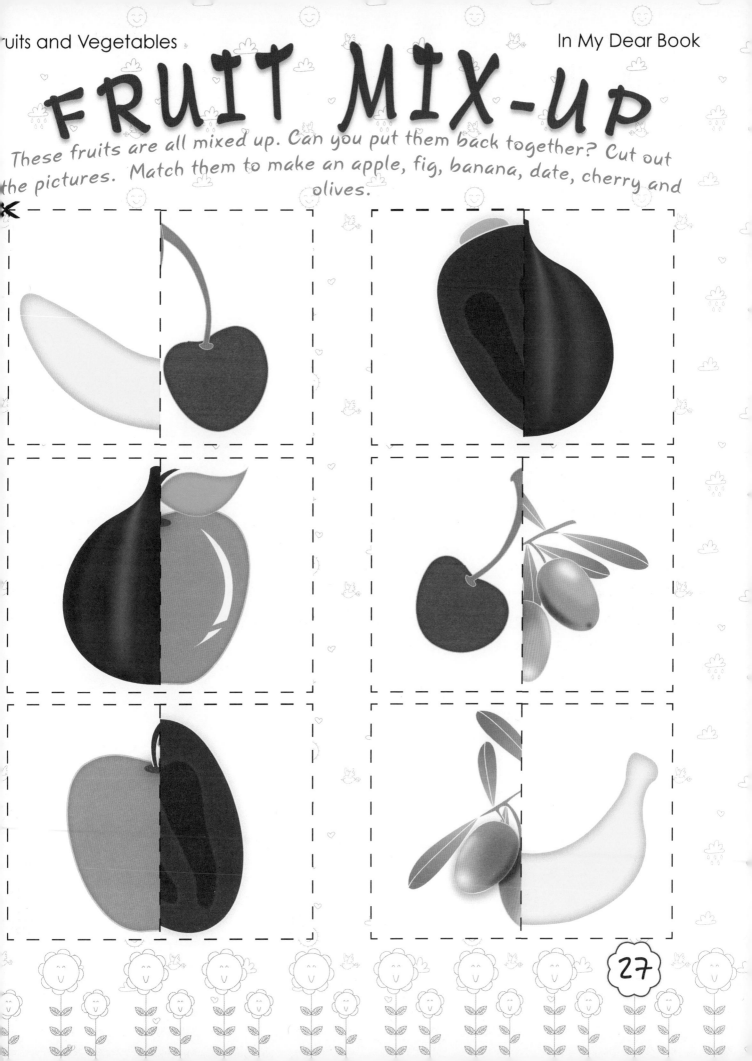

FUNNY FACES!

Can you draw faces to the fruits?

FIRST LETTER

Can you circle the first letters of each fruit and vegetable?

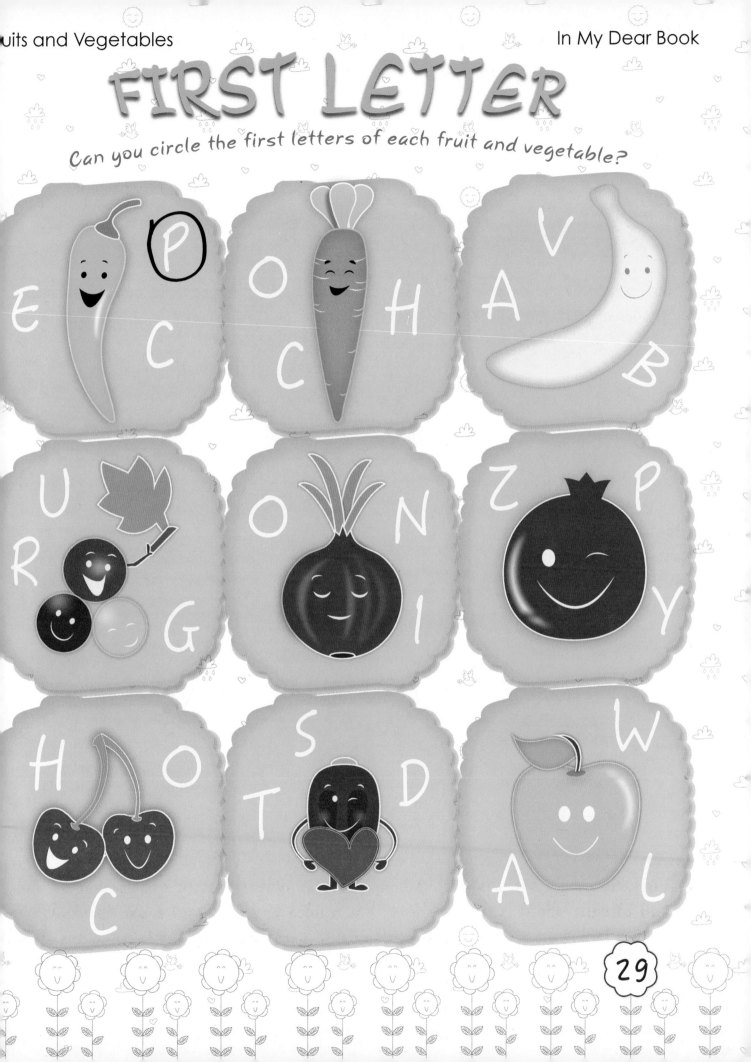

E P C

P O H C

V A B

U R G

O N I

Z P Y

H O C

S T D

W A L

Congratulations! You have reached the end of this book!

Allah (Subhanahu Wa Ta'Ala) has filled the world delicious and nutritious wonders just for our sake! These delicious and nutritious wonders, as you learned, are fruits and vegetables!

I hope after reading about all their benefits you realize the mercy and love Allah (Subhanahu Wa Ta'Ala) has bestowed upon us. Remember to thank Allah (Subhanahu Wa Ta'Ala) for all of the fruits and vegetables and not just the ones I mentioned in this book because they are all beneficial to us!

One day hopefully, I will also be able to teach you about garlic, lentil, pumpkin, basil, ginger...and the list goes on! What about meat, fish, milk, bread and water...surely these are important foods as well. Let's thank Allah (Subhanahu Wa Ta'Ala) for all of the foods he has created to help us grow and live healthy lives!

Try this tasty recipe from the author's sister who is also a chef!

THE DATEWICH
(Date Sandwich)

INGREDIENTS:

Date

Almond or hazelnut or cream cheese

HOW TO MAKE IT:

To make this recipe, you must first split the date, remove the seed and replace it with an almond, a hazelnut or cream cheese.

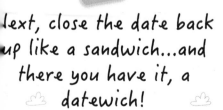

Next, close the date back up like a sandwich...and there you have it, a datewich!

Delicious right? Don't forget to make a datewich for me too please!

I do not have apple or fig trees, vineyards and beehives, but I could love to play toy with cherries, draw smiles on oranges and even build a house out of watermelons.

Did you know that all of Allah's fruits are mentioned in the Holy Quran? ... (Subhanahu Wa Ta'Ala) has created all of the fruits and vegetables in the world and each of them have their own unique shape, taste and colour. Fruits and vegetables give us the nutrients we need to work to grow big and strong.

I wrote this book because I wanted to thank ... (Subhanahu Wa Ta'Ala) for providing us with all of the fruits and vegetables through which we receive the nutrients we need to live a healthy life! While you read about these superstar fruits you will also want to thank ... (Subhanahu Wa Ta'Ala).

Fruitful reading,

Sajina Mart

Printed in Great Britain
by Amazon

37788769R10021